WATÁKAME'S JOURNEY

WATÁKAME'S JOURNEY
The Story of the Great Flood and the New World

HALLIE N. LOVE

A Huichol Indian Tale Retold
by Hallie N. Love and Bonnie Larson

ILLUSTRATED BY HUICHOL ARTISTS

CLEAR LIGHT PUBLISHERS
Santa Fe, New Mexico

DEDICATION
To my son, Tristan

ACKNOWLEDGMENTS

Special thanks to David Ross for his constant support, Jenifer Blakemore, Donna Collins, Patricia Lynn Sprott, and Rosemary Zibart for their reading of the work; also Robert Bovard, John Alderson, Carlos Sierra Valderrama, Hal Larsen, Carolyn Thomas, Kirsten Coglin, the Huichol People, and Marcia Keegan, Sara Held, and Carol O'Shea of Clear Light Publishers

Illustrations © by Guadalupe Barajas de la Cruz, Priciliano Carrillo Rios, Lusia Rios, David Gonzales Sanchez, Isadora Carrillo, Guadelupe Gonzalez, José Isabel Gonzalez, Fabian Gonzalez Rios, Abaristo Diaz Benitez, Modesto Rivera Lemos, and José Castro Villa

Clear Light Publishers
823 Don Diego, Santa Fe, NM 87501
web site: www.clearlightbooks.com

First Edition
10 9 8 7 6 5 4 3 2 1

Library of Congress Cataloging-in-Publication Data

Love, Hallie N. (Hallie Neuman), 1953-
    Watakame's journey : the Huichol myth of the great flood and the new world / Hallie N. Love : a Huichol tale retold by Hallie N. Love and Bonnie Larson : illustrated by Huichol artists.
        p. cm.
    ISBN 1-57416-029-X
    1. Huichol mythology. 2. Huichol Indians—Folklore. 3. Deluge--Folklore. 4. Huichol textile fabrics Juvenile literature.
I. Larson, Bonnie. 1942- . II. Title.
F1221.H9L68 1999
398.2'089'9745—dc21
                        99-14580
                        CIP

Jacket art (front) © by David Gonzales Sanchez
Jacket art (back) by unknown artist
Edited by Sara Held
Book design, typography, & production by Carol O'Shea

Printed in Hong Kong

Contents

The First World

IN THE EARLIEST TIMES when life first walked the earth, there lived an ancient race called the animal people. Some looked like animals. Others appeared to be people. Many were a changing mixture, part human, part animal.

In that first world there also lived a boy with a brave heart whose name was Watákame. He could change shape and color, but his form always remained human. He lived with his mother and father in the foothills of the Sierra Madre Mountains in Mexico.

Before sunrise, Watákame climbed into the mountains to find a place where he could plant corn. Bushes had grown thick during the summer rainy season. Watákame swung his sharp machete to clear a trail up the slopes.

Watákame struggled upward, slashing brush at each step. The first light of dawn warmed him. High in the mountains he pretended to soar like an eagle over the sun-painted canyons below.

Far away, he saw the roof of his family's house. It looked like a black speck among other tiny rooftops. Watákame had always lived in the village, but he was not happy there. The animal people were lazy and thoughtless. Every day they complained it was too hot to work, and every night they grumbled it was too cold to pray.

Watákame loved working in the mountains where he could not hear them. Often he would lift his eyes to the heavens. He wondered if there was another home beyond the clouds.

Watákame wore his stiff-brimmed, straw sombrero to shield his face from the now-searing sun. He carried his machete, his drinking gourd full of water, and his brightly colored, woven bag filled with sweet tortillas made from the corn he had grown and harvested last year.

Between the mountain peaks, Watákame saw a good place to plant. But it was wild with young trees and crowded with tall grasses and weeds. It would take all day to clear it.

Watákame climbed down to the plot. As he hacked the bushes, he worried, "What if the rains never come and the corn I work so hard to plant never grows?" Out of the corner of his eye, he saw a small black animal watching him. In a heartbeat it ducked behind a rock.

Pulsing, the sun moved across the sky. Not a single cloud sheltered Watákame from the fierce rays. Still, he cast blow after blow with his machete. Salty sweat streamed down his forehead and trickled into his eyes.

Blinking away the sweat, he swung the machete so hard he lost his balance. The machete's sharp blade cut Watákame's leg as he fell to the ground.

A voice in his head scolded him. "The machete punished you, because you neglected to feed it," the voice said. "Your machete is alive."

Watákame didn't listen. Only a few drops of blood trickled down his leg, but his pride was hurt. He was so angry he smashed the machete against a rock. Then he stomped it into the ground.

But he still had work to do. He seized the machete and whacked at the bushes. The blade was nicked, bent out of shape, and so dull that he now had to work twice as hard.

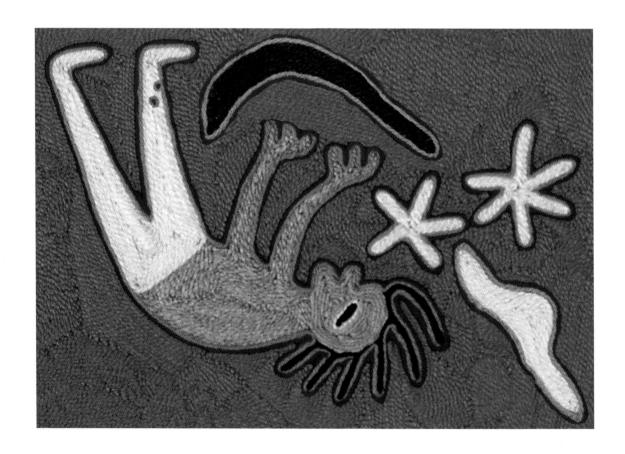

The small black animal appeared again. It scratched the earth, uprooting weeds Watákame had missed. When Watákame stood to get a better look, the animal disappeared in a ball of dust.

Watákame kindled a small fire to heat his lunch. The wind quickly snuffed the fire out. He lit the fire a second time. The wind blew it out. He tried a third time—no luck.

Watákame wondered, "Why does nothing go easily?" He ate his lunch cold, then worked all afternoon leveling the field—the soil was dark and rich.

At last crickets called and daylight dimmed. By moonlight Watákame stumbled over loose stones on the rugged path as he made his way toward home.

The second day Watákame scrambled up the rocky mountain trail. When he got to his field, he couldn't believe his eyes. All the bushes he'd chopped the day before had grown back overnight!

"What spell has undone my work?" he demanded. But no one was there to answer him.

He decided to repeat yesterday's work, but today he would feed his machete. He sprinkled it with cool water from his gourd and placed tortillas next to it.

When Watákame picked it up, the machete felt as good as new. It was light in his hand, and it seemed to help him as he slashed the bushes.

At dusk Watákame trudged home. The black animal pattered after him down the trail. Watákame saw that it was a little dog. He called her to come, but she streaked into the shadows of the cold night.

When Watákame arrived at his plot the third morning, it was overgrown with bushes again! So he toiled another full day, cutting down every single bush.

The same thing happened the next day and the next. On the fifth day, Watákame decided to wait patiently and see what magic would come.

He fretted when he realized he would need a fire to keep warm. However, this time, when he tried to light the branches, they caught fire! He stared into the flames. The fire soothed him and made him drowsy. He tried not to fall asleep. . .

The Goddess of Living Things

A STRANGE RUSTLING roused Watákame. He turned and saw an ancient, wrinkled woman with long, flowing white hair. With her staff, she prodded the bushes Watákame had chopped. As he watched, every branch she touched sprang back to life!

Watákame was furious to see all his work ruined. "Why are you doing this to me? Why are you bringing back everything I cut down?"

The old woman replied, "Be calm, my son. I undo your work because it is not time to plant."

"Who are you anyway?" Watákame wanted to know. "I should kill you," he threatened.

"I am Nakawé, goddess of all growing things. The animal people no longer deserve the gifts of the gods. They don't perform rituals or go to sacred places where the gods are hungry for offerings. They don't sing to us. We have been forgotten."

Watákame scowled at the old woman, but he knew everything she said about the animal people was true.

Nakawé said, "I am tired of feeding them. They live on my body, the earth. I receive nothing in return. Soon this will end. The Hakayuka sea monster will let the sea loose. All the thoughtless ones will perish in a great flood, but I will save you if you do as I say."

Watákame didn't want to hear such things. He ignored Nakawé and kicked up soot and ashes to smother the last coals of the fire.

Nakawé continued, "You must make a boat out of the mighty zalate tree that stands taller than any living thing. Make the roof tight to keep the water out. Gather grains of sacred corn. Collect bean and squash seeds and pick five squash stems. You will light one squash stem each day of the flood to keep fire alive. Your only companion will be a female dog. On the sixth day I will return."

"I can't build a boat," Watákame protested. "How can I make a roof?"

"You have five days. There is one more thing you must remember." Nakawé pointed her magic staff at him. "Tell no one of this."

In a flash, the old woman vanished.

Watákame called after her, "Why me? Find someone else to do all your hard work!"

Watákame ran down the mountain. In his mind he heard Nakawé's words over and over. He thought about how she brought bushes back to life. "I'm dreaming," he told himself. "When I wake up in the morning, the dream will be gone."

The next morning Watákame knew it wasn't a dream. His father pointed at the mountain. "It's still green," he said. "Why haven't you cleared a field?"

Watákame's mother scolded him. "Because of you we'll starve next spring."

Watákame ached to tell them something terrible was coming. But he remembered Nakawé's warning and said nothing.

Watákame neglected his chores. He sat outside and did not answer his parents when they spoke to him. He forgot to eat and muttered to himself. At night he lay awake in his bed.

His parents worried about him. They thought some sorcerer had stolen Watákame's soul.

For two days Watákame thought about the coming flood that would destroy the world. He thought about the tasks Nakawé had given him. He felt lost and alone.

That night he wandered away from his parents' house. He gathered wood for a fire.

The Fire God

WATÁKAME REMEMBERED it was good to feed the machete. Maybe it would also be good to feed the fire. He found a branch of dark red brazilwood and laid it on the struggling flames. Then they leaped high and crackled happily, devouring the wood. Watákame fed the fire more and more brazilwood until it was satisfied. He sat in front of the blaze and gazed into the heart of the fire.

Many colors flickered in the flames. Watákame saw fantastic shapes in the fire, and colorful patterns seemed to live and breathe, grow and shrink.

In the center of the fire, a grizzled old face appeared. Watákame realized it was the wise fire god himself, Tatewarí.

The fire god spoke. "Long ago," he said, "when the world was cold and dark, fire belonged to the gods alone. Men bribed Coyote to steal some of it. They promised to give him all the rabbits he could eat.

"Coyote found his way through the darkness to the gods' fire. He brought corn as an offering and sticks to feed the flames. He asked the gods, 'May I give you these in exchange for sitting by your fire?'

"The gods granted permission, and Coyote laid his gifts next to the embers. When no one was looking, he snatched hot coals in his mouth and fled. His mouth burned, but he did not drop the coals.

"The men tried to light a fire with the coals Coyote brought back to them, but nothing burned because the coals turned to stone. When Coyote demanded rabbits, the men laughed at him. Coyote never forgot how badly they treated him. Ever since, Coyote has played tricks on people whenever he's had a chance."

In the silence of the night, the fire popped. Tatewarí continued: "People may have gifts from the gods only if they show respect. Listen to the voice of fire, see with your heart, and you will become wise." Tatewarí's face dissolved into the flames.

Watákame watched the fire until it melted into ashes. He was no longer afraid because he knew the fire god would look after him. He knew he must follow the goddess Nakawé's plan. He must be especially careful to keep a squash stem lit so that fire would not be lost during the flood.

The flood! Watákame realized he had only three days left!

Building the Boat

WATÁKAME SLIPPED into his parents' house. He grabbed his ax and his woven bag and sped to the zalate tree. Before Watákame set to work, he sifted cornmeal onto the ax to feed it.

The zalate tree was huge. Leaves and flowers showered down as Watákame struck the bark with his ax, but the blow hardly nicked the tough tree. Hour after hour Watákame hacked the tree, until he finally made a gash halfway through the trunk. He braced himself in a wide stance and pushed. The tree did not budge. He shoved harder and strained until the tree leaned, leaned, and finally crashed to the ground!

With his ax, Watákame hollowed the trunk into a boat. He chopped a second tree and began to carve the roof.

Animal people passed by and gawked at Watákame. Two jaguars crept up to the boat and jumped inside, startling him.

The jaguars rocked the boat from side to side. "Where's he going to row this boat?" one of them asked. "Do you see any water?" The big cats laughed and rocked the boat so hard it flipped over. "Now see if it floats!"

Creatures with long tongues spat at Watákame as he struggled to turn the boat right side up. The spit splattered Watákame's forehead and shoulders. The creatures sneered, "Look at him. He's dirty. His clothes are full of holes."

Flying animal people with tattered feathers dived at Watákame and flapped their wings in his face. Then they flew off jeering.

A bull rammed the boat with his horns. Watákame cried out to the animal to stop. The bull butted the boat a second time. "Get away from here!" he bellowed. "You and your boat! Nobody wants you here!"

Watákame ignored the bull and continued carving the roof of his boat. The bull swung his shaggy head back and forth and charged off, snorting.

The little black dog had been hiding among the trees. When the animal people left, she came to Watákame.

He petted her. "I will follow whatever the gods tell me," he said. "Then things will turn out right."

The Quest

THAT NIGHT WATÁKAME dreamed of a magical deer spirit who leaped up to him and looked into his eyes. "My name is Kauyumári," the deer said. "I am here to guide you, but you must also look deep into yourself. Trust what your heart tells you." Kauyumári told Watákame he must search for deer in the hills and valleys. In the deer tracks he would find the sacred corn Nakawé told him to gather.

The next morning Watákame took his bow and arrows, gourd, and woven bag and wandered toward the mountains. The little black dog tagged along, chasing into the sagebrush after squirrels and lizards.

At last Watákame spotted a herd of deer through the trees. He followed them along a stream. The little dog leapt into the water, her legs flying. The deer galloped up the stream bank, leaving deep tracks.

Just as Kauyumári said, corn plants sprang up instantly in each
deer footprint. The kernels were white. Watákame gathered them
and put them into his bag. He explored deep valleys shaded by
trees and vines. There he found deer tracks bearing yellow corn
and he tucked the kernels into his bag. The little dog followed,
sniffing the ground.

Watákame and his dog tracked deer through the mountains,
where Watákame found red, spotted, and blue corn. He stored the
kernels in his bag.

Along the way, Watákame collected squash stems and seeds
and bean seeds and dropped them into the bag.

Everywhere Watákame traveled, the little dog was his faithful
companion. "You will come with me when the flood comes," he
told her. "And you will be safe."

Watákame wanted to thank Nakawé for her gifts of water to drink and fish in her streams to eat. He wanted to make her an offering, but he needed help.

Watákame looked up. An eagle soared high above him. Watákame lifted his arms, praying for its guidance.

The eagle answered by swooping low. Watákame shot his arrow, and the powerful bird spiraled to the ground. Watákame thanked the eagle for giving its life for an offering to Nakawé.

Watákame whittled a piece of red brazilwood into an arrow and fastened eagle feathers to the shaft. He wove yarn and sticks into a design. He attached it to the arrow as a prayer to Nakawé to help him see and understand unknown things.

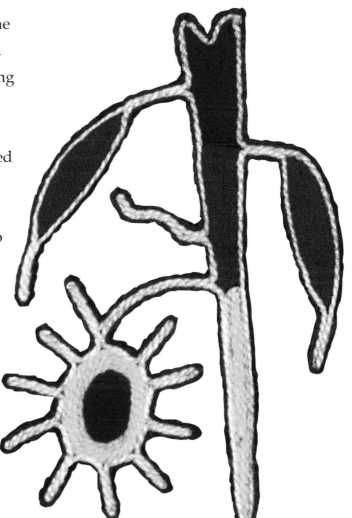

The Flood

WATÁKAME PLACED all the extra eagle feathers in his woven bag and hurried through the hills back toward the boat. The dog ran beside him.

Overhead mighty thunder rumbled while gray and black clouds wrestled. Howling winds raised whirlwinds and uprooted trees! Watákame ran faster, his heart pounding. Lightning split the sky! Heavy raindrops gouged pits in the earth. Splintered huts and torn-off roofs scattered in the wind. People were blown about like twigs.

When Watákame reached the boat, the little dog was nowhere in sight. He whistled and shouted, but the dog did not come. "I can't wait for you!" he wailed.

He tried to light the first squash stem. The strong wind blew out the flame. Watákame worried. He tried again, but now the squash stem was soaked with rain and wouldn't burn.

Suddenly the dog darted into view.

She was frightened of the thunder and refused to come when Watákame called. He lassoed her with a rope.

Lightning struck the trees nearby! Fires erupted! The little dog bolted into the boat!

Stepping into the boat, Watákame gripped the wet squash stem. He must light it somehow! Desperately he raised the stem and prayed toward the four directions—north, south, east, and west—and to the fifth direction in the heavens. Lightning blasted from the sky and struck the squash stem—it lit! Watákame slid inside the boat, sheltering the flame.

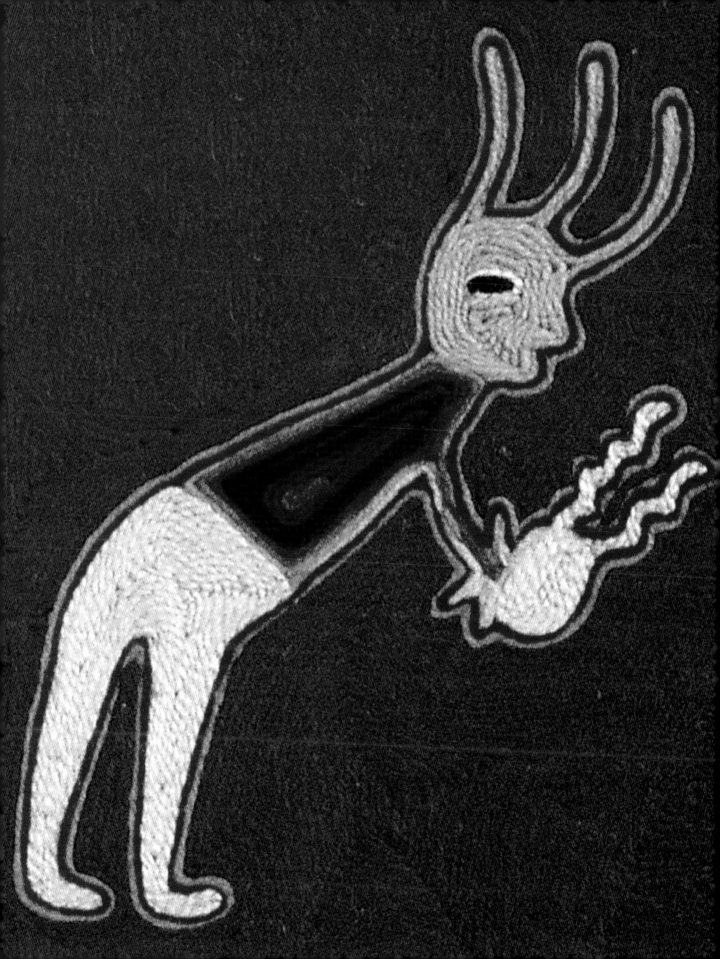

The waters rose rapidly, and rivers of mud flowed down the mountains. If the boat didn't cast off soon, it would be buried.

Nakawé appeared, carrying an oar. She looked inside the boat to see that Watákame had brought the seeds, the lighted squash stem, and the little dog. "It is for this moment that you were born," she said.

Nakawé fastened the roof of the boat and sat on top. With her oar, she launched the boat into a huge wave as a tide of mud from the mountains churned into the swelling water, barely missing the boat!

Outside their little house, Watákame's mother ran through the rain screaming, "Watákame, where are you? Help us!"

His father called, "Watákame, come back!"

But Watákame was already far away.

Dark clouds wrapped the sun and the waters rose higher.

As Nakawé predicted, the Hakayuka monster burst from the sea! Enormous waves lashed across the land, sweeping away the villages of the animal people, sweeping away rocks and mountainsides and every living thing.

Nakawé paddled hard in the battering winds. Ferocious waves heaved the boat into the center of the sky. Watákame held the squash stem carefully and comforted the little dog. "Nakawé's magic will keep us safe," he told her.

Each day, Watákame transferred the flame to another squash stem so fire would not be lost in the great storm.

Nakawé opened the boat's roof a crack, so that Watákame could glimpse the flooded world.

Watákame saw the animal people who had taunted him. Human birds with tattered wings flapped across the water and were pelted with rain until they drowned. The bull floated by, his head barely above water, gasping for air until the waves pulled him under. The bodies of the spitting creatures drifted lifeless in the water's froth.

The last cries of the beings who had roamed the first world faded in the water and sank into silence. The rain was transformed into serpents that swam by, gorging on the remains. Only sticks and branches floated in the swirling water.

The sun weakened, the days were dismal, the moon was cold. The sun sank, sizzling into the ocean.

Watákame and the little dog crouched inside the boat for five days and five nights. The only light was the glow of a single burning squash stem.

Watákame peered out of the boat. Over the earth lay a vast ocean dressed in empty blackness. Suddenly colors burst through the darkness. Watákame's heart beat wildly. Bright-colored snakes rippled in the black water.

Watákame saw Kauyumári, the spirit deer, breathing lightning. Beautiful five-petaled flowers turned into corn of different colors. Candles and prayer arrows flew through the air. Gods carrying lightning rose from the deep water. Some of them walked across the foam of the sea, some vanished into the clouds. Others spun from the black ocean as whirlwinds. The magical sights filled Watákame with wonder.

The New World

ON THE SIXTH DAY, Nakawé moved the rain gods far into the sky and the storm quieted. The spirit of the old sun rose from the depths as a majestic eagle, its feathers shining like gold. With a fierce beating of his great wings, the eagle ascended into the heavens and transformed into the fiery new sun god! His rays bathed the new world in brilliance. Clouds were wreathed in his light.

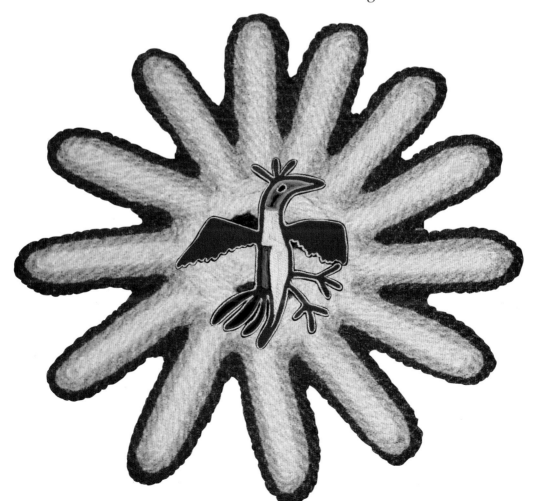

Nakawé steered the boat to a mountain that jutted out of the water. She said, "The world has been remade."

Nakawé opened the boat. Shivering with cold, Watákame stepped onto the land. He squinted in the bright sunshine.

With her magic staff, Nakawé created three birds: the turkey, the rooster, and the quail. She told them,"Go now and give the sun a name."

Each of the birds wanted to name the sun. The rooster and the quail argued.

"Ta-ta-ra-riii!" the rooster crowed.

The quail replied, "Rruuuuu."

In his own language the turkey quietly gobbled, "Tau, Tau."

The new sun god listened to the birds and decided to choose a name himself. He was most pleased with the modest turkey, so he took the name "Tayaupá," which sounded like the turkey's gobbling.

Tayaupá told Watákame, "I will help you, if you remember to bring me offerings and gifts."

Watákame removed his bag of seeds and the last burning squash stem from the boat.

Nakawé said, "With the seeds from your bag every plant will grow. In five days I will recreate all life."

The little dog shivered and refused to get out of the boat. She sniffed the air curiously. Finally she jumped from the boat into the unknown.

The pure winds lifted Watákame's hair. His footsteps left tracks in the soft ground. Never had Watákame felt such thankfulness!

Kneeling on the ground, Watákame sifted the dirt through his fingers. "The soil is dark and rich," he thought. He imagined a field with gleaming rows of ripening corn.

Watákame remembered how hard he had worked to plant corn for himself and his parents. Loneliness crept into his heart, and a tear rolled his cheek. The little dog licked it away.

Nakawé said to Watákame, "It is time for you to discover what your life will be. I have work of my own to do." Nakawé took seeds from Watákame's bag and set off to a cave where she made her home.

Watákame, still carrying the lighted squash stem, sloshed along a rain-soaked path with the little dog. They came to a sheltered spot.

Watákame stopped. "This will be our home," he announced. He stashed the squash stem in a sheltered place between two rocks.

He patted mud into bricks and let them dry in the hot sun until they were hard as stone. With these adobe bricks he built a one-room house with thick walls. He placed the doorway facing east to greet the rising sun. He wove long reeds through bunches of dried grass and tied them in overlapping bundles to make a thatched roof.

Inside the house Watákame dug a deep, circular hole. Then he brought the burning squash stem into the house and placed it in the hole. He added wood. Sparks leaped to the timber, and flames shot up. The fire god Tatewarí was finally home!

While Watákame built his house, the little dog explored. She returned carrying something in her mouth—a stick of dark red brazilwood from the last creation! Watákame carved it into an arrow.

The eagle feathers in Watákame's woven bag moved as if they had a life of their own. They wiggled out of the bag and flew to the arrow he had just carved! Watákame quickly caught them and tied them in pairs to the neck of the arrow. The feathers twitched as if trying to talk.

Watákame knew this arrow with special powers must be a gift from the gods.

Watákame was exhausted from building the house. He lay down to sleep on the dirt floor, his little dog nearby.

He dreamed that he was walking alone through the desert. It became dusk, then dark. He made a fire. In the flames he saw the familiar wrinkled face of the fire god, Tatewarí.

Tatewarí said, "It is time for you to journey to a sacred place in the desert called Wirikúta. There Kauyumári, the deer spirit, will teach you to be a shaman."

Tatewarí's image faded, and the antlers and face of the deer spirit emerged.

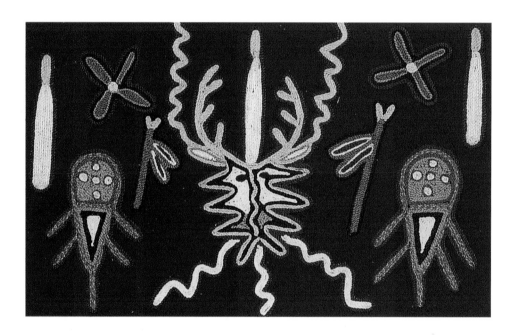

Tatewarí continued: "You will gain knowledge of healing. In your dreams and visions, you will soar like the eagles and talk to the sun god, the wind god, and the rain goddesses. Your special arrow will be your shaman's wand of power. It is called a *muviéri*. Tomorrow at sunrise, you must use it to bring your ancestor spirits to the new world."

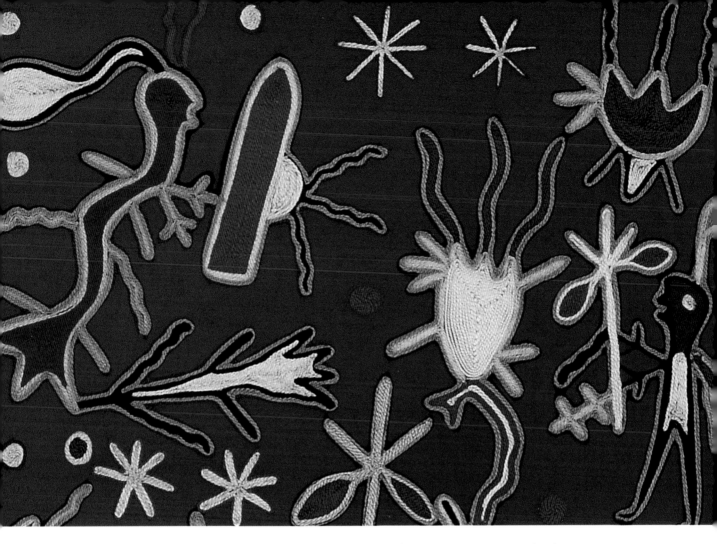

Watákame woke. It was moments before sunrise. He rushed outside and faced east. Holding the *muviéri* in his hand, he prayed to the sun. As the sun spread his light across the earth, the eagle feathers on the *muviéri* vibrated with some mysterious force.

Watákame saw shimmering stones travelling on the rays of the sun. The stones were snatched from the air. When Watákame looked closely at his *muviéri*, he saw that two small rock crystals were tangled in the eagle feathers!

Excitedly he took the treasure into his house to show the little dog. Watákame exclaimed, "Look! These are the souls of my mother and my father. They have returned to me as beautiful crystals!" Watákame reverently wrapped the crystals in small squares of cloth and tied the bundle to an arrow.

Journey to Wirikúta

WATÁKAME PREPARED for his journey to Wirikúta, where he would learn to be a shaman. He packed the muviéri, the rock crystal souls, and offerings of gourds, flowers, and incense. He made several prayer arrows to bring with him. He invited his dog to come, but she preferred to stay at home in comfort.

Watákame set off across a landscape of jagged mountain ridges and sun-parched deserts. The sky had no end. For five long days he walked, guided by the dancing feathers of the *muviéri.*

He found the entrance to Wirikúta, a dark shaft in the ground blocked by boulders and guarded by coyotes. Watákame shrank back in fear when they howled at him. Then a voice came out of Watákame, singing. At first the coyotes could think only of the wicked tricks men had played on them in the past. But Watákame's song was pure, and it charmed them into opening the passageway.

Watákame passed through a twilight tunnel and emerged in a magic land. Ahead of him was a mountain of many-colored rocks covered with sweet-scented flowering sage.

Watákame climbed to the top of the mountain. He lit incense and candles. He kindled a fire, and placed his prayer offerings on a mat in front of it. Watákame held the long slender staff of his *muviéri*.

He looked into the flames, and as in his dream, he saw the antlers and head of the deer spirit.

The fire god, Tatewarí, spoke. "Kauyumári sees, hears, and knows all. He moves between the worlds of humans and gods."

Suddenly the full form of Kauyumári surfaced from the fire and stood before Watákame.

Tatewarí said, "In the god realm there is much you will not understand. Kauyumári will translate for you and be your messenger. Listen to him through your *muviéri*. Follow the instructions Kauyumári brings and the gods will look after you."

Kauyumári's form disappeared.

Watákame listened to Kauyumári through the *muviéri*. He heard messages from the gods! In the morning Watákame chanted a song Kauyumári had brought him from the gods.

Over several days, Watákame learned how to leave the earth and travel to other worlds in visions and dreams. He learned what prayers and offerings needed to be made to the gods for good rainfall and crops, healthy children, abundant animals, and protection from harm.

Watákame learned about *niérikas* — colorful designs with circles in the centers. The circles were holes into other dimensions. Through the holes he could look into the god realm and the gods could look out.

After Watákame listened to the gods' messages for five nights and five days, it was time to return home. The coyotes watched Watákame leave and locked Wirikúta behind him.

Watákame and Yokawima

ON HIS JOURNEY HOME, Watákame noticed new life everywhere and knew that Nakawé had remade it with her magical staff. She had created birds of many colors and sculpted tall trees that swayed in the wind. She had formed deer, lizards, and squirrels that dodged into holes as Watákame walked by.

At home, Watákame's dog bounded to greet him.

"It's almost time to plant," Watákame said as he petted her. First he had other things to do. Next to his own house, Watákame built a smaller dwelling he called a god house, where the gods could visit and where the crystal souls of his mother and father would live forever.

In front of the god house, Watákame made an altar of bamboo poles tied together with fibers. There he placed offerings to the gods. Watákame also made a three-legged drum, which he put inside his own home.

The following morning, Watákame got up early and sharpened his machete. He packed his tools and offerings, and filled his gourd with water. He walked until he found a good place to plant high on the mountain.

Watákame made a little fire, and all day he cleared the plot with his machete. When the fire burned low, Watákame fed it plenty of wood so Tatewarí would guard him. He did not worry that the rains would not come. He did not fret that he might not have enough to eat. He trusted that the gods would look after him.

At home after work he carried his machete and ax to the god house. Watákame knew his tools were alive and that they often felt hunger. He sprinkled them with corn and water.

Watákame went to his house, thinking, "My stomach aches too. It is so empty."

To his surprise, he found fresh, warm tortillas waiting for him. Watákame looked inside and out for someone who might have made them, but he found no one. He gratefully gulped the tortillas down, saving some for his dog.

Every day Watákame went to work in his field, and each night when he arrived home, he found tortillas!

One day while Watákame cleared his field, he heard the sharp crack of twigs underfoot. He spun around . . . it was Nakawé.

Watákame told her that every night when he returned home he found fresh tortillas. "Who made them?" he asked.

"You are now a man," Nakawé said. "Go home now and hide yourself. See what happens."

"Then what?" he asked her.

She raised her magic staff. "You will know what to do," she whispered.

Watákame left the field early that day. When he returned home he hid outside the doorway. He was amazed to see the dog take off her black pelt and lay it on the floor! The spirit of the dog rose like a human and started to grind corn for tortillas!

Watákame rushed into the house and flung the dog's pelt into the fire. The dog's spirit fell to the ground. As the pelt burned, the spirit cried out that her skin was on fire! Watákame doused the weeping spirit with water.

The spirit stopped crying. When she stood up, she was a woman!

Watákame's eyes widened in pleasure the instant he saw her, and he fell in love. He knew he had to have her for his wife.

Nakawé arrived and gave them her blessings. She named the woman Yokawima and told the couple that they would be the parents of a new race of people, the Huichols.

Yokawima loved Watákame. She made tortillas for him every day. She went to the spring with her gourds, filled them, and brought water to Watákame in the field. Watákame and Yokawima placed offerings in the center of the field to the goddess of the moist earth, Utuanáka. Yokawima said, "As the soil gives us food to eat, so we must nourish her."

Now it was time to plant. With a digging stick, Watákame poked holes in the dirt. Yokawima followed, dropping corn, squash, and bean seeds in the holes. They planted five colors of corn in five directions on the steep mountain slope. Then they gave offerings to the corn goddess, Niwétsika.

A Time of New Beginnings

NOW WATÁKAME needed to call the rain mothers to the mountains so the seeds would sprout. He needed to summon Nu'ariwaméi, the rain god of lightning and thunder. Watákame knew what to do. Kauyumári had taught him well. He made a fire and beat his three-legged drum, softly at first, then louder and louder until the drum's reverberations shook the sky. Then he pointed his *muviéri* in the five directions and chanted.

Kauyumári took Watákame's request for rain to the gods. When Kauyumári came back he told Watákame what offerings the gods wanted. "Nu'ariwaméi, the rain god of lightning and thunder, desires a picture of a sea monster," he said. "Nakawé, the goddess of life, wants agave cactus, a lizard, and a model of the boat you made in the first world. The rain mothers and the wind want prayer arrows, gourd bowls with sacred symbols, *niérikas*, and candles."

Watákame gathered the cactus, caught the lizard, and made all the other offerings. He placed them on the altar outside the god house.

The rain goddesses called their spirit animals. They called on the rain serpent. They called on the salamander, who stirred up the clouds. The rain mothers called all their children in the heavens. The rain god shot down bolts of lightning with his bow and arrows and spat raindrops from his mouth.

The gods unleashed torrents of rain that streamed down like a million snakes falling from the sky.

After the rains came, the first shoots of corn broke the soil. Watákame and Yokawima worked hard to rid the field of weeds that tried to choke Niwétsika, the corn goddess. Soon the mountain slopes gleamed with the light green of new corn. Before long, corn stalks twice the height of a man rustled in the wind. Bean plants grew around the stalks, and squash plants fanned out on the ground.

Watákame and Yokawima bore children. Their children had children, and those children had many more. From Watákame and Yokawima all Huichols have descended.

The First Shaman

WATÁKAME TAUGHT the people of the new world the rituals and ceremonies the gods required. He reminded his descendants to treat the earth with care. He taught the Huichols to take offerings to sacred places—to the cave where Nakawé lives, to the Pacific Ocean where the goddess Harámara lives, and to Wirikúta where Kauyumári lives.

Watákame told stories of the gods—for they are Huichol history—of the end of the old world and the creation of the new. He taught the people how to sing and chant so nothing would be forgotten and the gods would preserve the new world. Watákame selected shaman apprentices with brave hearts and taught them the secrets Kauyumári had revealed to him.

Watákame could see ahead for generations to come. He saw the spirits of the unborn Huichol children lighting candles in the sky, filling the night air with sparkling lights.

Harvest Festival

IN THE FALL when the corn was tall and ripe, the field was harvested, and the corn festival began.

The crystal souls of Watákame's mother and father and the other ancestors were brought out and fed.

To please the gods, the people decorated their hats with feathers and painted their faces.

The people honored and fed Tatewarí. They placed offerings for all the gods on the altars. To the beat of a wooden drum, they chanted. Watákame heard the gods' voices and repeated their songs.

The Huichol people sang and danced and thanked the gods for the harvest of corn that would feed them through the year.

To this day, the Huichol people remember the gods. They recite the sacred myths and chants from the time of the ancestors. Prayers float up into the sky in the Huichols' mountain homeland in Mexico.

Illustrated Glossary of Huichol Symbols

Shaman's Objects

Shamans are spiritual leaders. Huichols believe shamans have supernatural powers and can see into the god realm and talk to the gods.

Muviéri - Shaman's wand of power made of a red brazilwood arrow with a pair of eagle feathers attached to it. A shaman uses his muviéri to communicate with the gods.

Niérikas - Colorful designs with circles in the centers. The circles are holes into other dimensions. Through the holes a shaman can look into the god realm and the gods can look out.

Drum - Used in ceremonies, aids in communication with the gods. A hollowed-out log with a deerskin head.

Prayer arrow - When given to the gods these arrows express gratitude or payment for requests.

Spirit Animals

 **Kauyumári** - Deer spirit guide, leads shamans on their spiritual journeys and teaches them knowledge of healing.

 Rattlesnake - Spirit animal of the fire god, Tatewarí. Its rattle is the tongue of Tatewarí.

 **Salamander** - Spirit animal of the rain mothers. It stirs up the clouds to make rain.

 Snakes - Spirit animals of the rain goddesses. Huichols believe that rain is made of millions of small snakes.

 Eagle - Spirit animal of the sun god. The sun god is often called "Werikúa," which means eagle.

 Turkey - A magical animal of the sun. The sun god's name "Tayaupá" is from the turkey who gobbled "tau, tau."

Gods and Goddesses

Huichols have many gods and goddesses and many different names for each one. The few deities listed here appear under these names in this book.

Goddess of Life, Nakawé - Creator of all living things.

Fire God, Tatewarí - Teacher of the shamans.

Sun God, Tayaupá (or sometimes called **Werikúa**, which means eagle) - Ensures good crops and abundant food.

Goddess of the Pacific Ocean, Harámara - Sends rain clouds to Huichol country.

God of Lightning and Thunder, Nu'ariwaméi - Shoots lightning from his bow and arrow and spits rain from his mouth.

Goddess of Corn, Niwétsika - Responsible for the five colors of corn—white, red, yellow, spotted, and blue.

ABOUT THE HUICHOL INDIANS

HUICHOL INDIANS live close to nature in the rugged Sierra Madre mountain area northwest of Guadalajara, Mexico. Relatively isolated from the outside world, they have proudly sustained over a thousand years of indigenous ways.

Huichols still use machetes and digging sticks to grow corn on the steep slopes of the Sierra. Corn is sacred food, and a great deal of Huichol ceremonial life is aimed at safeguarding the crops.

Religion permeates every aspect of Huichol life. Huichols still live by the rituals required by the gods from the beginning. Their religion stresses communication with the spiritual world and harmony within the natural world. Huichols believe all beings and all things must be of one heart to ensure the continuation of life.

For the Huichol people, the ancient myths are the stories of real events. It is vital to the survival of the culture that the chants and myths be told over and over, so that nothing will be forgotten and Huichols will always know their history and follow their customs.

The illustrations created for *Watákame's Journey* are the work of more than eleven Huichol artists. The artists create images by pressing colorful yarns into softened beeswax and pine pitch that have been applied to a wood panel. Symbolic yarn paintings are not considered to be sacred objects in themselves. Rather, they illustrate and record the sacred ancient myths that represent the history of the Huichols.

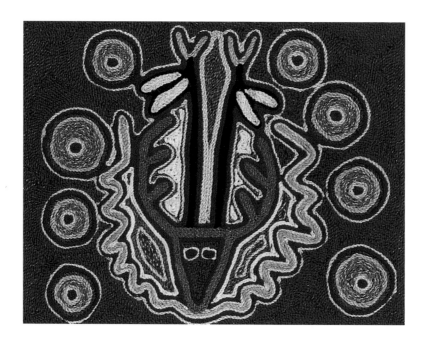